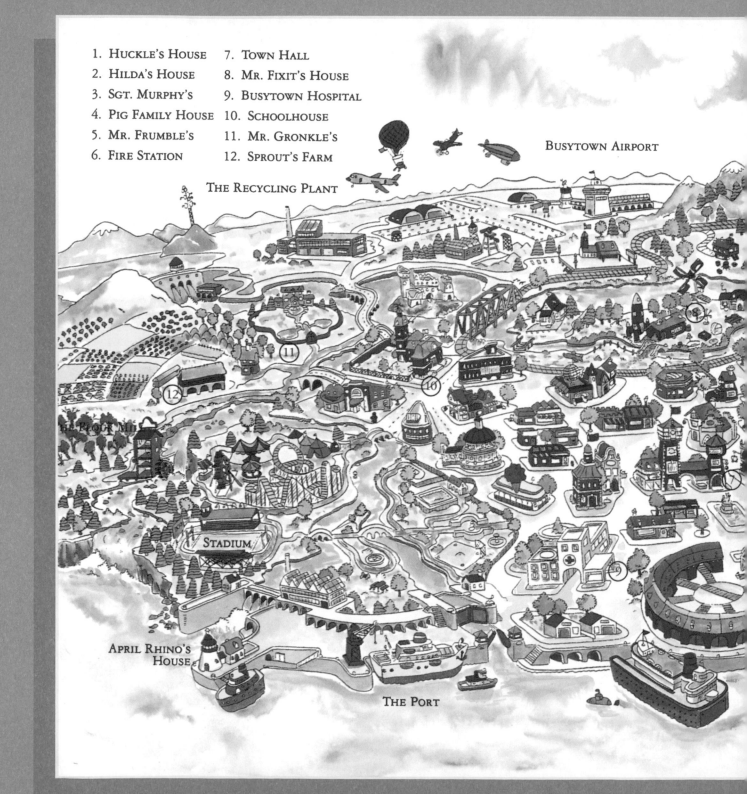

1. HUCKLE'S HOUSE
2. HILDA'S HOUSE
3. SGT. MURPHY'S
4. PIG FAMILY HOUSE
5. MR. FRUMBLE'S
6. FIRE STATION
7. TOWN HALL
8. MR. FIXIT'S HOUSE
9. BUSYTOWN HOSPITAL
10. SCHOOLHOUSE
11. MR. GRONKLE'S
12. SPROUT'S FARM

BUSYTOWN AIRPORT

THE RECYCLING PLANT

THE FLOUR MILL

STADIUM

APRIL RHINO'S
HOUSE

THE PORT

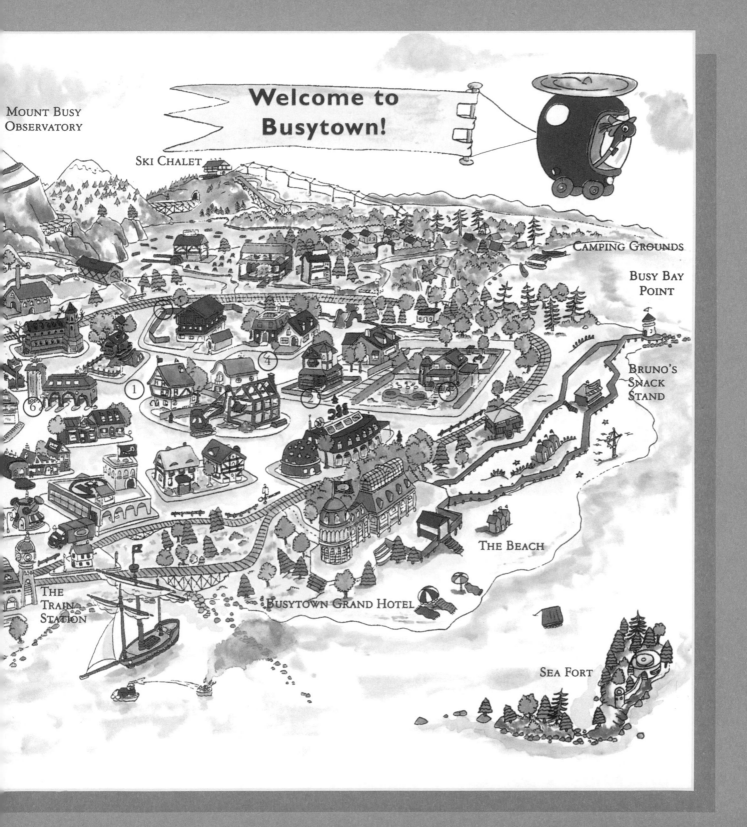

This book
belongs to:

....

The Busy World of Richard Scarry

The Best Story Collection EVER!

LITTLE SIMON

New York   London   Toronto   Sydney

LITTLE SIMON
An imprint of Simon & Schuster Children's Publishing Division
1230 Avenue of the Americas, New York, New York 10020
A Big Operation, The Snowstorm, Camping Out, The Treasure Hunt,
and *Mr. Frumble's New Cars* copyright © 1994 by the Estate of Richard Scarry. Compilation
copyright © 2004 by The Richard Scarry Corporation. Adapted from the animated television
series *The Busy World of Richard Scarry* produced by Paramount Pictures and Cinar.
All rights reserved, including the right of reproduction in whole or in part in any form.
LITTLE SIMON is a registered trademark of Simon & Schuster, Inc., and
associated colophon is a trademark of Simon & Schuster, Inc.
Manufactured in the United States of America
First Edition 10 9 8 7 6 5 4 3 2 1
ISBN 0-689-87839-7

These titles were previously published individually by Aladdin Paperbacks.

Table of Contents

Camping Out

Father Cat is raking the leaves on the lawn. **BANG!** goes the kitchen door. Huckle and Lowly rush inside the house.

"Hi, Mom," Huckle says. "Lowly and I are going camping!"
"Oh, really! Where?" Mother Cat asks.
"Well, we wanted to go to Africa," Lowly says, "but that's too far. So tonight, we'll just camp out in the backyard."

"Can we borrow a sheet for our tent?" Huckle asks his mother.
"Of course, but take an old one from the drawer."
Huckle whips out a patched sheet. Ooops! The sheet falls over Lowly.
"Great!" he exclaims, popping out from a hole. "Here's a window!"

Father Cat leans his
rake against a tree.
"Whew! I could use
a rest," he says.

As he goes into the kitchen, Huckle and Lowly dash out, yelling,
"Quick! Let's pitch our tent!"

"So you're going camping!"
Father Cat looks at them
and smiles.
He turns to Mother Cat.
"I remember the first time I
camped out in my backyard.
My mother gave me her
oldest sheet for my tent too.
I was so scared that night!"

Mother Cat is worried.
"Do you think Huckle and
Lowly will be all right?"
"Oh, of course! I'll show them
how to make a safe campfire
that should keep any wild
animals away!" says
Father Cat.

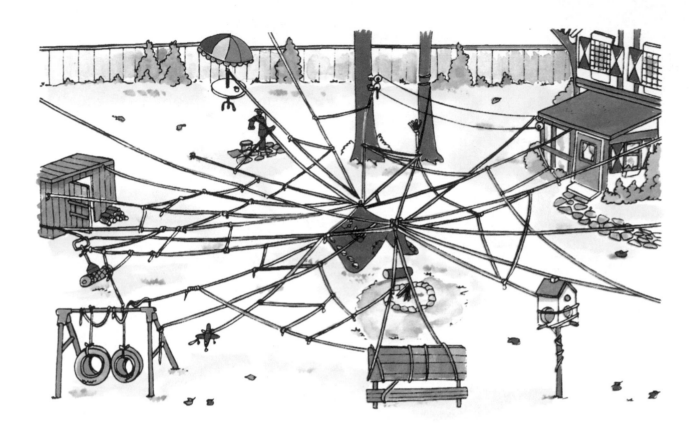

In no time, the two boys have pitched their tent.

18

Mother Cat comes out of the kitchen with her laundry. And Father Cat comes out of the shed with a big pile of firewood in his arms.

Look out, Father Cat!
Whoops!
Poor Father Cat!

"These ropes have to come down, Huckle!" Father Cat says.

"But what about our tent?"
Huckle asks.
"Don't worry," his father
says. "I'll show you how
to pitch a tent properly."
Father Cat helps Huckle
and Lowly put the tent
up, and shows them how
to build a proper campfire.

"Remember, Huckle, always keep your fire away from grass and trees.
And don't forget to put stones around it. That way the fire won't spread.
And before you go to bed, make sure you put the fire out."
"Wow, Dad," Huckle says. "You know everything!"

That evening, Huckle and Lowly toast marshmallows over the campfire.
"This is the life, Lowly," Huckle remarks.

Suddenly, they hear a loud cracking sound.

They both jump up, terrified.

Lowly hides up Huckle's sleeve.

The bushes glow with light. What can it be?
"Maybe it's a wild animal... come to get our marshmallows," Huckle says.
"Or maybe it's come to get us!" whispers Lowly.

Just then, Kenny Bear pops
out from behind the bushes.
He lowers his flashlight and
walks over.
"Hi, Huckle. Hi, Lowly!"

Lowly quickly slides out from Huckle's sleeve.
"Hi, Kenny!" they reply. "We were pretending
you were a wild animal!"

They all sit down by the campfire.
"Would you like a marshmallow?" Huckle asks.
"Thanks!"
"Oh, Kenny," Huckle says, "do you
know any good ghost stories?"
"Yes, I know a really good one.
Do you want to hear it?"
"Oh, yes, please, Kenny!"
the boys say.

"Well, it's called 'The Tale of the Ghostly Claw,' because the ghost has this great, big, hooked claw..." Kenny tells Huckle and Lowly his spooky story...

"...And they say that on nights like this, you can hear the screams of his victims...

...'Ah! Whoooo will save me from this ghostly claw'?"

Kenny smiles. "I can see I scared you."
"Ummm... what makes you think that?" Huckle asks.
"You're eating your stick, that's why," Kenny replies, laughing.

Mother Cat opens the kitchen door and calls, "Kenny! Your mom wants you to go home."

"Well, good-night," Kenny says. "Sleep well. And watch out for the Ghostly Claw!"

"Maybe it's time we went to bed too,"
Lowly whispers to Huckle.

"OK. But remember what Dad told us
about making sure the fire is out."

Huckle pours a bucket of water on
the fire. A huge cloud of smoke rises
in the air and disappears into the night.
"It's a lot darker without the fire,
isn't it... Lowly?" Huckle says.

But Lowly has disappeared! Poor Huckle, he's never been so scared in all his life! He dives into the tent and pops out at the other end! So that's where Lowly was hiding!

"I wonder whether it gets this dark in Africa," Lowly remarks.

Huckle and Lowly get into their sleeping bags.

"Well, Lowly, here we are, camping out. It's fun, isn't it?"
But before Lowly can answer, the friends hear a little trickling noise.
Plink! Plink!
Huckle turns on his flashlight.
"Who's there?" he asks, putting on a brave voice.
"Maybe it's the ghost..." Lowly trembles.

Nearby, water drips from the well.

Squeak! Squeak!
Lowly and Huckle are terrified.
They peek outside.

But it's just the pulley of the
clothesline squeaking!

They smile at each other.
"Now, let's get some sleep!"
Huckle says.

Huckle and Lowly snuggle down
in their sleeping bags.
Both begin to nod…
Suddenly, Lowly shouts,
"Huckle! Look!"
A big claw-shaped shadow is
trembling on the wall of their
tent.

"Let's get out of here!" yells Huckle. They scramble out of the tent and run as fast as they can back to the house.

Early next morning, in Huckle's
bedroom, the two campers
sleep peacefully.
Huckle wakes up first.
"Pssst! Lowly," he says.
"It's time to get out of bed."
"Huh? What is it?" yawns
Lowly, sleepily.

"Shhh! We don't want to wake up Mom
and Dad. Let's go back to our tent."

They both slip outside quietly and
get into their sleeping bags.
"Good-night again, Lowly," Huckle
says before closing his eyes.

Mother Cat and Sally come outside with some breakfast.
"Good morning, Huckle, good morning, Lowly!" Sally calls.
"Did you sleep well? Were you scared?"
"Um… uh… no…" Huckle replies.
"And you, Lowly?"
"Me? I slept like a log," Lowly answers bravely.

Huckle and Lowly join the family for breakfast at the picnic table.
"Good morning, boys," says Father Cat. "I think you are very brave
staying out all night. I remember the first time I went camping, I was
really scared."
"Oh? What scared you?" the boys ask.

"I must admit, it was rather silly. I was scared of a shadow! It looked like a big claw... but it was only the shadow of a rake!"

Huckle and Lowly eat their cereal quietly.

36

Mother Cat turns to Huckle and says, "As soon as you have finished breakfast, you had better start packing for your next camping trip. You said you were going to Africa, didn't you?"

"Ummm..." Huckle replies, "Lowly and I have been thinking about it..."

"And we decided," adds Lowly, "that there is no finer place to camp out than your own backyard!"

A Big Operation

Huckle doesn't feel very well this morning.
He has a sore throat. Dr. Lion has come to examine him.
He listens to Huckle's heartbeat.
"How does it sound, Dr. Lion?" Lowly asks.
"Hmmm, you have a fever, Huckle. And this is your third
sore throat this year, isn't it?" remarks Dr. Lion.

"I think Huckle should have his tonsils taken out," Dr. Lion says.
"Does that mean he has to go to the hospital?" Mother Cat is worried and so is Huckle.
"You're not scared, are you, Huckle?" Sally asks.
"Oh no," says Huckle. His voice is very hoarse.

"Don't worry, Huckle," says Dr. Lion. "I'll take you and your family on a grand tour of the hospital before we check you in."

The hospital is a very busy place.
Look! Here comes an ambulance!
"Stand aside, everyone!" call the ambulance men.
"It's an emergency!"

It's Mr. Frumble!
"Oh, good morning,
Mr. Frumble," says
Nurse Nora. "We've
reserved your usual
room."
"Hello, Nurse Nora,"
Mr. Frumble answers.
"I'm afraid I fell on
my nose again, chasing
my hat."
"Well, I'm glad you
found it," says Nurse Nora.

Dr. Lion takes the Cat family
on a tour of the hospital.
First they visit the operating
room.

Just look at all that equipment!

Huckle, Sally, and Lowly are impressed.

Then Dr. Lion takes them to another room.
"This is the X-Ray Department," he announces.
They enter the darkened room.

46

"Yikes!" Sally shouts. "They've got skeletons in here!"
"They are not spooky skeletons, Sally," Dr. Lion explains.

"These are X-ray pictures of patients who are treated in the hospital. People like Mr. Frumble."

"Look, here's Mr. Frumble's broken nose!"

"Can we borrow this machine for Halloween?" asks Sally.
"I don't think so, Sally," Dr. Lion answers.

Dr. Lion takes them outside into the garden.
"Hospitals aren't so bad after all," Huckle says.
"I'll have the operation, but can Lowly stay with me?"
"Of course he can," says Dr. Lion.
"We will have such fun!" Lowly exclaims.

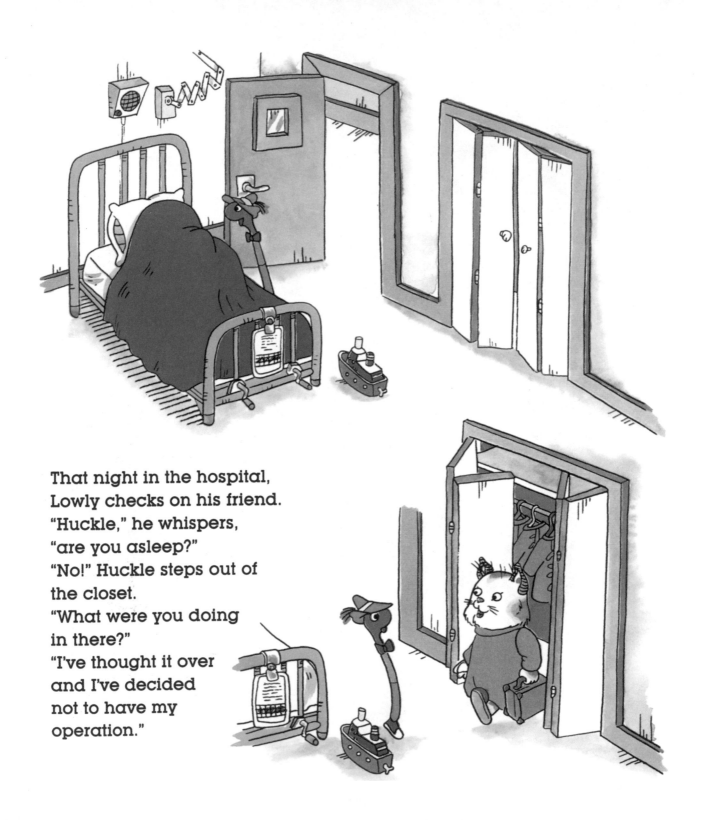

That night in the hospital,
Lowly checks on his friend.
"Huckle," he whispers,
"are you asleep?"
"No!" Huckle steps out of
the closet.
"What were you doing
in there?"
"I've thought it over
and I've decided
not to have my
operation."

Huckle leaves the room, taking his suitcase with him. "Huckle, are you leaving because you're scared?" Lowly asks.
"Scared? Me? Ha!" laughs Huckle. "Well, maybe just a little..."

"Listen, Huckle. I have an idea. Maybe if you talk to some of the other patients you will feel a bit better. Let's go see Sprout Goat."

"Hi, Sprout. Why are you in the hospital?" Huckle asks.

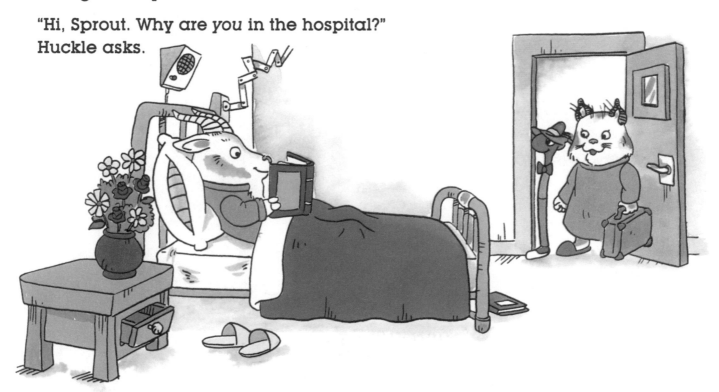

"I'm here for another operation to straighten my leg. It's the fourth and last time," Sprout explains.

"You've been here four times and you're not scared!" Huckle is amazed.

"I was at first, but the nurses are so nice..."

"But don't the operations hurt?"

"A little bit, afterward," Sprout says, "but you sleep right through the operation and don't feel a thing."

"What are you in for?"
Sprout asks Huckle.
"To have my tonsils out."
"Oh! You are lucky!"
exclaims Sprout. "After
the operation, you will
get ALL the ice cream
you can eat!"
"Wow!" says Lowly.
"Ice cream sounds good,
but I'm still leaving,"
says Huckle.

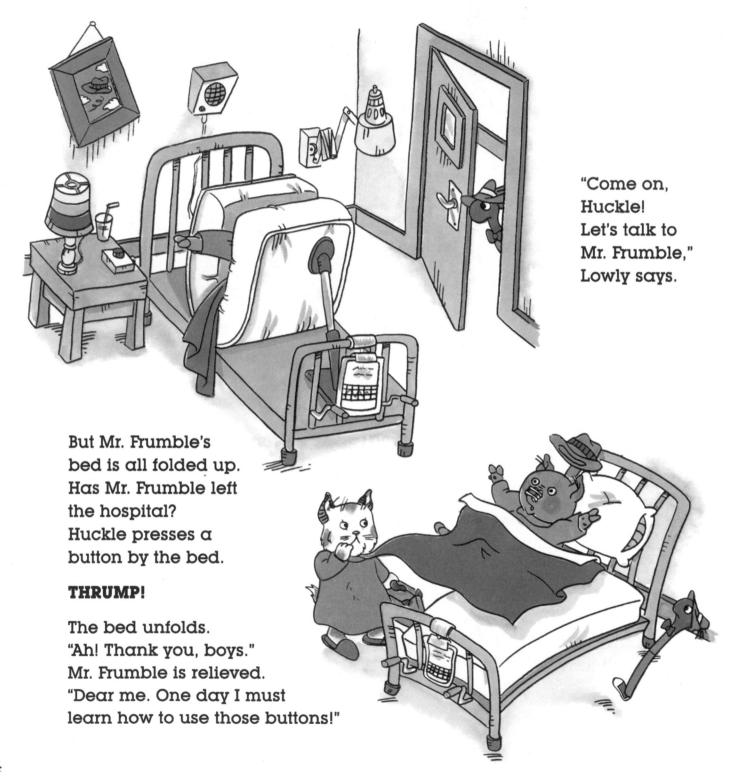

"Come on,
Huckle!
Let's talk to
Mr. Frumble,"
Lowly says.

But Mr. Frumble's
bed is all folded up.
Has Mr. Frumble left
the hospital?
Huckle presses a
button by the bed.

THRUMP!

The bed unfolds.
"Ah! Thank you, boys."
Mr. Frumble is relieved.
"Dear me. One day I must
learn how to use those buttons!"

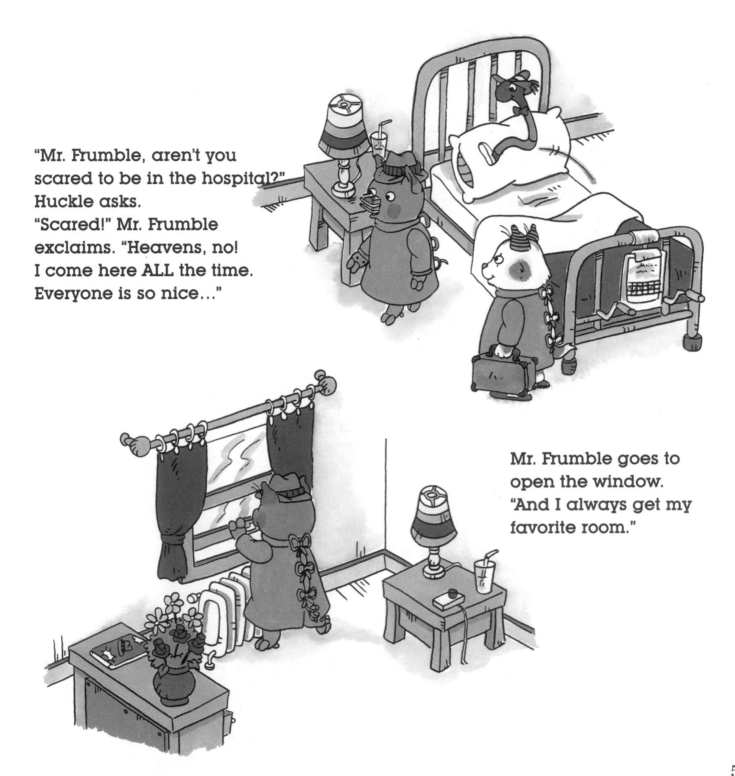

"Mr. Frumble, aren't you scared to be in the hospital?" Huckle asks.
"Scared!" Mr. Frumble exclaims. "Heavens, no! I come here ALL the time. Everyone is so nice..."

Mr. Frumble goes to open the window. "And I always get my favorite room."

"Sprout and Mr. Frumble need to be in the hospital.
They have real problems. All I have is a little
sore throat," says Huckle. "I'm leaving!"

Just then, Huckle sees a friend of his.
"Oh, Mrs. Stitches! What's wrong
with you?" he asks.
"Nothing at all, boys. I have
a new baby and this hospital
is taking the BEST care of
both of us."

Nurse Nancy comes in holding Mrs. Stitches's new baby. The baby giggles in the nurse's arms. "Well!" Lowly exclaims. "SHE certainly looks happy to be here." "Hmmm..." says Huckle, thoughtfully. "If a little baby isn't afraid to be here, I guess I shouldn't be either!"

Huckle decides to go back to his room.

The next morning, Huckle is
brought to the operating room.

He is very quiet.

Dr. Lion takes out a mask and says to Huckle, "Try to count backward from one hundred."

"OK," Huckle says and he begins to count:
"One hundred, ninety nine, ninety eleven, ninety eight…mmm…mm…"
In a moment, the special gas has put Huckle to sleep.

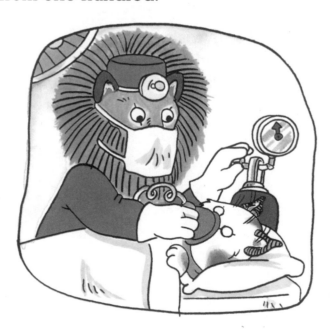

"Huckle? Huckle, are you all
right?" Sally asks.
Huckle slowly opens his eyes and
whispers, "Ninety seven... Hey!"
He looks around at his friends.
"What are you all doing here?"
"The operation is over," Father Cat
says. "You have been asleep
for hours..."
"How do you feel, darling?"
Mother Cat asks.
"My throat is still sore,"
Huckle replies.

"Hey, Huckle! How about a little ice cream?" suggests Lowly, jumping on the bed.

Huckle takes a spoonful and swallows. Ow! It hurts!

"Hey, Sprout. You said I could have all the ice cream I can eat!" Huckle protests.

61

"No, I said all the ice cream you *could* eat!" says Sprout. "But I can see you can't eat any just yet!"

"Well," says Lowly, taking Huckle's spoon, "if I ever have MY tonsils out...

...you can eat all MY ice cream. I promise!"

The
Treasure Hunt

"Ahoy, mateys! On yonder isle be the buried treasure. And THIS be our only map!"

Miss Honey is reading a pirate story to Huckle's class.

"Did those pirates ever come back for the treasure?" Lowly asks.

"I am afraid we'll have to wait until tomorrow to find out." Miss Honey closes the book. "School is over for today."

"Oh no!" says the class, disappointed.

Huckle and Lowly stay behind after
class. Huckle wants to ask Miss Honey
a question.
"Miss Honey, do you think there
is any treasure buried here in Busytown?"
"Well, Huckle, in the olden days pirates
could have sailed into Busy Bay."

"Maybe we can find their treasure!" says Huckle.
"I bet they buried it on the beach!" Lowly adds.

"Just remember, boys,"
Miss Honey says, "we
don't always recognize
treasure when we see it!"

Later that day, Huckle and Lowly go down to the beach,
dressed like pirates. They meet Mr. Fixit on the boardwalk.
"Yikes, pirates!" he shouts.
"Don't be afraid, Mr. Fixit. It's only us," Lowly says.

"We are on our way to find some buried
treasure," Huckle explains. "Then we will
have enough money to buy our own pirate ship."
"But there is one small problem," Lowly says.
"We're not sure where to dig…"
"Well," says Mr. Fixit, "in the old stories,
X always marked the spot."

"Oh, look! There's an X over there!"
Huckle shouts. "Bye, Mr. Fixit.
Come on, Lowly, let's get to work."

"Yo-ho-ho!"
"And here we go!"
"How deep do you think they buried their treasure?" Huckle wonders.
"At this rate, we'll be in China soon!" says Lowly, exhausted.

Suddenly, Huckle's shovel hits something hard. **KLANK!**
"Lowly, I have hit metal! It sounded like gold!"
"Klank? Is that what gold sounds like?" Lowly asks.
"Oh, it's silver, Look, it's a silver goblet!"
"It looks like it sprang a leak," Lowly says.
"Oh no!" says Huckle, disappointed. "It's just an old tin funnel."

"No wonder we didn't
find any treasure,"
says Huckle,
looking around.
"We didn't dig
under the X!
The X is over here.
This is the right spot!"

KLONK!
"Did you hear that sound, Lowly?"
"Doesn't silver go klonk?" Lowly asks.

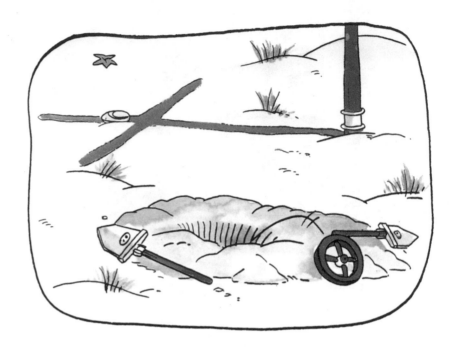

"Yes, you're right," answers Huckle. "But this is far too big to be a silver coin. Oh no! Look! It's just an old wagon wheel..."

"...I don't think we'll find any treasure here."

"Oh, look, Lowly! That shadow keeps moving because
the sun keeps moving!"
"I bet this drove the pirates crazy!" Lowly replies.
"Well, that treasure must be here... somewhere."

Mr. Fixit thought he would
see how Huckle and Lowly
were doing.
"So, what have you found,
mates?" he asks.
"Well, it wasn't treasure,"
Huckle says, pointing at
a heap beside him.
"Look at all that junk,
Mr. Fixit!"

"An old beach umbrella,
a towel, a doll, someone's
T-shirt, some old rope..."

"I wouldn't call that junk!" says Mr. Fixit. "Do you mind if I borrow this stuff?" "You are welcome to it, Mr. Fixit," Huckle says. "We've finished hunting for treasure!"

"Well, Lowly," Huckle sighs, "we can forget about buying our own pirate ship." "Do we have enough money for ice cream?" Lowly asks. Huckle looks in his pockets. "Uh-oh, not a penny!" he says. "We're pretty poor pirates, aren't we?"

Huckle and Lowly walk over to Bruno's snack bar.
They both feel sad.
"No luck?" says Bruno. "That's rough. But you know, boys, I can tell you
how to find some *real* treasure."
"Really?" Lowly asks. "How?"

"If you take this box and pick up any trash you find
on the beach, I think I might be able to help you."

"Oh, well!" Huckle says.
"It beats digging."

Meanwhile, Mr. Fixit is busy in his workshop.

"Hmmm... these boys can't recognize treasure when they see it."

81

Mr. Fixit looks around for just the right tool
to work with. "Hmmm... let's try this one."
He takes a big mallet from the wall.
WHACK!

"Voilà!"
says Mr. Fixit.
CRASH!
"Oh dear!"
The wagon is
in pieces!

Mr. Fixit thinks hard.
"Ah-ha!" he exclaims happily.
He has had an idea!
He takes a broom and sets to work
repairing Huckle's wagon.

"Boy! Bruno has a funny idea of what treasure is!" Huckle says, placing the last piece of trash in Bruno's cardboard box.

"Hey! You boys have done a wonderful job!" Bruno exclaims. "I've never seen the beach so clean!"

"But where's the treasure?" Huckle asks. "There in your hands, Huckle," Bruno replies.

"All these old cans
and bottles can be
recycled and made
into new things,"
he explains.
"And your reward
for tidying up the
beach is... two ice
cream cones!"

Bruno hands two big cones
to the boys.
"Wow! Thanks, Bruno!" they say.
"Thank YOU!" Bruno replies.

Just then, Miss Honey arrives at the beach. "Well, how are my favorite pirates?" she asks. "And how did your treasure hunt go?"

"Oh, Miss Honey! You were so right!" Huckle exclaims. "We don't always recognize treasure when we see it!"

"Ahoy, you there on the shore! Are you ready to cast off?" calls Mr. Fixit, rolling Huckle's wagon down the boardwalk.

"Our pirate ship!" cries Huckle. "Mr. Fixit, how did you do it?" Lowly asks.

"As I always say, Lowly, one person's junk is another person's treasure!" Mr. Fixit answers wisely.

"Your ship awaits, Cap'n."
Mr. Fixit salutes Huckle.
"Wow!" cries Huckle, taking the helm.
Lowly jumps into the crow's nest.
"Ready to raise anchor, Cap'n?"
"Cast off yer bowlines!" shouts Huckle.
He proudly steers his new pirate ship
along the boardwalk.

Huckle and Lowly are very lucky pirates,
wouldn't you say?

The
Snowstorm

DRING!

It's time for recess at the Busytown school.
"It's very cold outside," Miss Honey
warns the children. "So don't forget
to dress up warmly."
The children can't wait to get outside.

They rush to the coat rack,
put on their coats, scarves, and
gloves, and off they go!

"Don't forget to pay attention
to your new playground monitor,"
says Miss Honey as they leave.

She turns to Hilda.
"Put on this vest so the
children will recognize you.
Do you feel ready for your new
job, Hilda?" Miss Honey asks.

"Yes, yes, I think so." Hilda squeezes the ball nervously.
Pop! The ball bursts!

"Sometimes I forget how strong I am, Miss Honey."
"Well, Hilda, you are stronger than the average girl."
"I'm afraid I'm stronger than TEN average girls!" answers Hilda.

Hilda walks over to the door and...**WRENCH!**
"Ooops! Excuse me, Miss Honey.
You see what I mean?"

In the playground, Sally and Nancy are playing catch.
Sally throws the ball to Nancy, but Hilda catches it and
throws it back... **Boom!** Poor Sally!

The ball knocks her over...

...and sends her flying into Sprout's sand castle! **WHAM!**

Poor Sally—she's buried deep in the sandbox! Hilda rushes over.

"Are you all right, Sally?" she asks, pulling her out by her legs.
"Yes, yes, I think so..." Sally catches her breath. "But I think I'll just have a little rest."

"Hilda, can you push me, please?" Kenny calls from the swings.
"I'm on my way, Kenny."

Hilda pushes Kenny gently.
"Higher, Hilda," he cries.
"Give me a BIG push!"

So Hilda gives him a BIG push.
Whoa!
Kenny flies through the air,
looping-the-loop, and lands
in the snow.
THUMP!

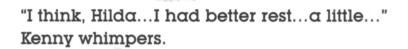

"I think, Hilda...I had better rest...a little..."
Kenny whimpers.

"Hey, Hilda!" Huckle calls
from the merry-go-round,
"Would you give us a spin?"
"I don't know if I should,"
Hilda sighs. "You never
know what might happen."

"Oh, please, Hilda!"
"We want to go faster!"
"All right," Hilda says. "But just a little spin."
"Oh no! We want a BIG spin!"
"All right, get ready!"

Hilda gives the
merry-go-round a push.

WHOOA!
There goes Arthur—goal!
There goes Bridget—goal!

The merry-go-round drills
deep into the ground.
"Slow down!" shout Huckle
and Lowly.

"Oh, what have
I done?" Hilda cries.

Huckle and Lowly pop out from the hole.
"Wow! That was some ride!" says Lowly.
"I didn't know a merry-go-round could spin so fast," Huckle gasps.
Recess is over and the children go back to their classroom.

The moment they are indoors, it starts to snow.
"Children, I've heard on the radio that there's going
to be a big snowstorm," Miss Honey tells the class.
"School will close now, so you can get home safely."
"Hooray!" the children shout.

"Oh! Look at all that snow!" the children gasp as they get on the school bus. Hilda decides to walk home, alone.

"Why didn't you get on the school bus?" Miss Honey asks her.

"Oh, Miss Honey. I'm too strong and everyone is afraid to play with me. I can't be a monitor anymore."

"Your strength is a gift, Hilda," Miss Honey answers gently. "You just need to learn how to use it."

The bus moves slowly down the slippery road.
It snows harder and harder.

"Can't we go any faster?"
Huckle asks Spotty Leopard,
the bus driver.
"No, Huckle, it wouldn't be
safe. We have to take it nice
and slow."
But even so, the bus skids
out of control.
It breaks through the
road barrier...

CRASH!

...and comes to rest in a ditch.

"Is everyone all right?" Spotty asks.
"Yes, we're all right!" the children shout.

"There's no need to be alarmed.
We're stuck in the snow and we'll just
have to wait in the bus until someone sees us."

Outside, it grows dark. In the bus, it's very cold. The children shiver and rub their hands together to keep warm.

Meanwhile, Hilda makes her way home through the snowdrifts.

Suddenly, Lowly notices
something moving outside.
"Hey, Huckle, look! Do you
see what I see?" They look
through the window.
"There's something orange
coming toward us...
...It's Hilda!"

"Hilda!" calls Spotty. "Am I
glad to see you! Can you go
and get help, please?"

"No, wait, Spotty, I have an idea.
Quick! Everyone out of the bus!" she orders.
Once the children and Spotty are safely outside, Hilda
grabs hold of the bus and lifts it out of the ditch.

"Hooray! Hooray! Bravo!" all the children shout. "That was amazing!"

"Wow!" Huckle says. "You're even stronger than I thought."
"Oh! It was nothing." Hilda blushes.
"Are you kidding? It's the greatest thing I ever saw in my life!" says Huckle.

The next day at school, Miss Honey reads the Busytown newspaper out loud to the class:

"Hilda Hippo's courage and strength saved the day, and her classmates awarded her a medal for heroism."

"Hooray for Hilda!" the children cheer.

DRING!
The bell rings
for recess.

The children run to
collect their coats and
scarves. They can't wait
to go and play in the snow!

Hilda walks to the door which Janitor Joe has just repaired.

CRUNCH!

WRENCH!

"Oops!" says Hilda, holding the door. "I've done it again!"

"Come on, everyone," she calls. "Let's go and play!"
"Yippee!" shout the children, running outside.

Poor Janitor Joe!

Mr. Frumble's New Cars

Mr. Frumble drives his pickle car through Busytown. Suddenly, a gust of wind blows his hat off. "Oh dear!" says Mr. Frumble, looking behind him. His hat is hooked on the tail of his car. He reaches out for it. "Ooops! Ahhh!"

Oh no! Look out, Mr. Frumble!
HONK! HONK!
Crassshhh!

"Don't worry, Mr. Frumble,"
Mr. Fixit assures him.
"I'll fix your car so that
it's better than new."

Sergeant Murphy
arrives at the
scene. "I'm sorry,
Mr. Frumble, but
I have to give
you a ticket.
It's the law."
"Oh dear,"
mutters Mr. Frumble.

UMFF!

Later that day, Mr. Frumble goes to Mr. Fixit's workshop.

"Your pickle car is ready, Mr. Frumble," Mr. Fixit says. "Well, thank you, Mr. Fixit."

Just then, Roger Rhino arrives in his bulldozer. His bulldozer needs a new scoop. "New scoop!" Mr. Fixit says. "I've got one in the back of my workshop." He turns to Mr. Frumble, "Why don't you take your pickle car for a test drive? You won't even recognize it!"

121

Mr. Frumble walks over
to the pickle car.
"But I recognize this car!"
exclaims Mr. Frumble.

"It can't be mine—Mr. Fixit told me I wouldn't recognize it!"
Then Mr. Frumble sees the bulldozer.
He climbs on the
seat, starts it up,
and drives away.

"My goodness!"
he says. "I certainly
don't recognize
this one."

Nearby, Sergeant Murphy is helping people cross the busy street.

VROOM!
Watch out, Sergeant Murphy!

He jumps out of the way just in time. That was a close call!

"Help! Help, Sergeant Murphy!" shouts Roger Rhino.
"Mr. Frumble has taken my bulldozer!"
"He can't drive the bulldozer any better than he can drive his pickle car!" Sergeant Murphy says. "I'll have to give him another ticket!"

"Hmmm...I wonder what all these handles do..."
Mr. Frumble pulls and shoves. Clonk! Watch out! Mr. Frumble puts the
scoop down. **OOOOOPS! CRASH!** The scoop has dug up the street!

"Dear me!" Mr. Frumble exclaims. "Who put this big pile of dirt here?"

Soon a big crowd gathers on the square.
"What's happened?"
"Who dug this big hole?"
"Are they building a new town hall?"
people wonder.

What is everyone looking at? thinks
Mr. Frumble, walking toward a car
nearby.

He climbs
inside and
closes the
door.
Hilda hasn't
noticed that
her taxi has
a new driver!

Mayor Fox calls Sergeant Murphy from his office. "Get down here fast! Mr. Frumble just bulldozed the town square and has taken off in a taxi!"

"Oh no, now I have a taxi to catch!" Sergeant Murphy says, speeding away, his siren blaring.

Mr. Frumble looks at the taxi meter.

"What a noisy clock Mr. Fixit has installed. I better go back and get it fixed."

"But I need to go to the airport!" Hilda shouts.

"Hilda Hippo!" Mr. Frumble exclaims. "What a surprise."

"Mr. Frumble?" she says, puzzled. "I have to meet my cousin in ten minutes!"

"Well, in that case we had better step on it!" Mr. Frumble makes a U-turn and speeds away in the opposite direction.

CRASSHH! The car leaves the road.
Mr. Frumble drives through the fence to the airplane
and right up the loading ramp.

"AHHHHHHH!"
Hilda screams,
running away.

"I wonder where Hilda went," Mr. Frumble mutters.
Meanwhile, Rudolf von Flugel lands his airplane.
"Why is everyone in such a hurry?" Mr. Frumble wonders,
climbing into the driver's seat.

Up, up,
and away
he flies!

"Mr. von Flugel, have you seen
Mr. Frumble?" Sergeant Murphy
asks, arriving on his motorcycle.

"He just took off in my plane!"
Rudolf answers.

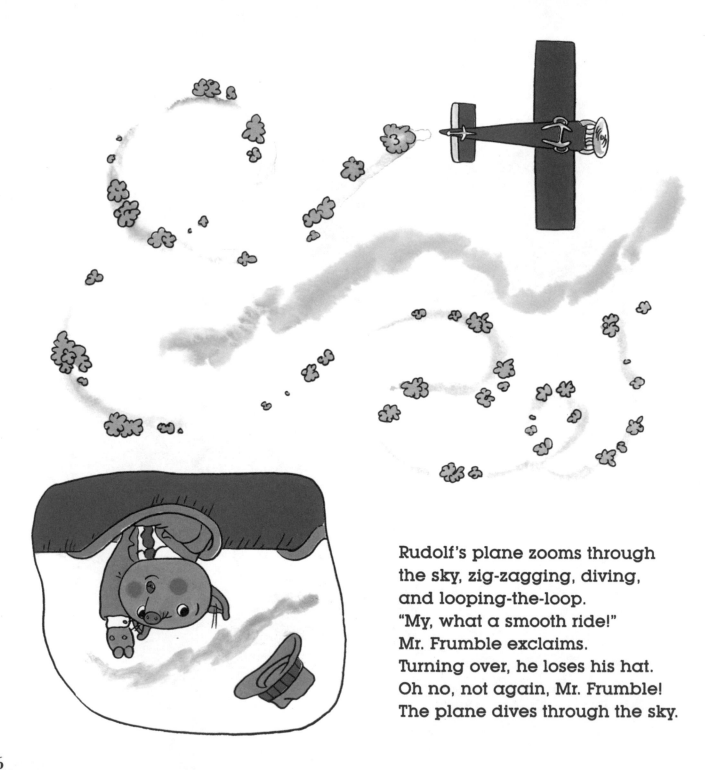

Rudolf's plane zooms through
the sky, zig-zagging, diving,
and looping-the-loop.
"My, what a smooth ride!"
Mr. Frumble exclaims.
Turning over, he loses his hat.
Oh no, not again, Mr. Frumble!
The plane dives through the sky.

"Now who would put a tree in the middle of the road?" wonders Mr. Frumble as the plane crashes through the branches. **THWASH!**

Mr. Fixit runs up.

"Mr. Frumble! Are you all right?"

"Yes, Mr. Fixit," says Mr. Frumble, hanging from a branch. "Fine, thank you."

BUMP! THUMP! Down comes Mr. Frumble! And down comes his hat.

"Mr. Fixit," says Mr. Frumble, getting up, "do you remember you told me I wouldn't recognize my car? Well, I wonder if you could fix my car so I COULD recognize it?"

"I tried to tell you before," answers Mr. Fixit, pointing. "Your pickle car has been here all the time!"

SCREECH!
Sergeant Murphy pulls
up on his motorcycle.
"Now that I've caught up
with you, Mr. Frumble," he
says, "I have a few tickets
to give you!"
Sergeant Murphy pulls
out his ticket book:

"This one's for failure
to stop for an officer…
This one's for digging
a hole without a permit…
This one's for illegal
tree trimming…"

...and this one's for littering."
Poor Mr. Frumble!
"Dear me, I think I will go now," Mr. Frumble sighs.
He climbs into the driver's seat one more time.

"Wait! Mr. Frumble!" Sergeant Murphy shouts.

140

"That's MY motorcycle!"